RED
AND THE
CITY

MARIE VOIGT

OXFORD
UNIVERSITY PRESS

Great Clarendon Street, Oxford OX2 6DP

Oxford is a registered trade mark of
Oxford University Press in the UK and in certain other countries

Text and illustration copyright © Marie Voigt 2018
The moral rights of the author and artist have been asserted

Database right Oxford University Press (maker)

First published 2018

Data available

ISBN: 978-0-19-276774-5 (hardback)
ISBN: 978-0-19-276687-8 (paperback)

1 3 5 7 9 10 8 6 4 2

Printed in China

Special thanks

Peter Marley

Stephanie Thwaites

Graham Tombs

Once there was a girl named Red,
who lived with her mum and her dog, Woody,
on the edge of the city.

'Red,' said her mum one day.
'Go visit Grandma and give her this cake.
Take Woody with you and remember—

Follow the heart flowers . . .

DON'T
WALK

'take care when crossing the road . . .

'stay on the path . . .

'and
don't
talk
to
anyone.'

After a while, Red started feeling hungry.
'I will only have a little bit of cake,' Red said.

But the cake was very tasty.
And before Red knew it, she'd eaten it all.

'Oh no, I've eaten my present for Grandma,' said Red.
'What shall I do now?'

'I know! I'll buy her some heart flowers.
They're not far from the path. I'll be back in a minute.'

TOYS

THIS
NEW

But Red quickly
forgot about the flowers . . .

'Ahhh . . .'

'Ohhh . . .'

'Mmmm...'

long

Before

Red was lost.

'Oh, city,
what shiny toys
you have!'

'All the better
to dazzle
you with.'

'Oh, city,
what shocking
news you have!'

'All the better
to worry
you with.'

'Oh, city,
what tempting
food you have!'

'All the better
to sicken
you with.'

And then

Red was swallowed up.

'Wake up! Wake up!' barked Woody.

And when Red opened her eyes,
she remembered all that truly mattered to her.

Her heart shone brightly
and she was able to find her path.

zzz zzz zzz zzz

And Red walked straight to Grandma's
without straying from her path once.

'Oh, Grandma, I'm so sorry I'm late.
I was foolish and got lost in the city.'

'I know,' said Grandma.
'It once swallowed me up too.'

They then ate the cake
Grandma had baked for Red earlier that day.
And they talked about all the wonderful things
they could do in the city together.

'Once there was a girl named . . .'